to Rena, Nina, Anneliese and Aunt Rose

KIM THÚY has worked as a seamstress, interpreter, lawyer and restaurant owner. *Ru* is her first book, has been published in 15 countries and received several awards, including the Governor General's Literary Award. Kim Thúy currently lives in Montreal, where she devotes herself to writing.

SHEILA FISCHMAN is the award-winning translator of some 150 contemporary novels from Quebec. In 2008 she was awarded the Molson Prize in the Arts. She is a Member of the Order of Canada and a chevalier de l'Ordre national du Québec. She lives in Montreal.

Rebecca, Margaret, and Nasty Annie

Story and Pictures by Jody Silver

Platt & Munk, Publishers/New York

A Division of Grosset & Dunlap

For as long as anybody could remember, Rebecca and Margaret lived upstairs from Nasty Annie, their landlady. Rebecca and Margaret were very old and had learned to be good to one another.

Many times when Rebecca went out, she would bring home a little something for Margaret.

And Margaret would often do the same for Rebecca.

They filled their room with treasures. After a while, it got so that it was hard to find their beds.

One day, when Margaret was out, she saw the loveliest stone vase. She tried to pick it up, but, alas, it was too heavy.

So even though it would spoil the surprise, she went home and told Rebecca.

Together, Rebecca and Margaret carried the vase up the stairs past Nasty Annie's.

They set it down with a great thud, which caused a bit of the ceiling below to fall, breaking Nasty Annie's teacup.

Nasty Annie rushed upstairs, pushed open the door, and said, "You broke my teacup."

When she saw the vase and all the other old things, she yelled, "Get rid of this junk, or I'll get rid of you."

Now, Rebecca and Margaret loved their treasures.

But they had no choice except to get rid of most of their things.
After all, they did not want to move.

Neatly, they placed their treasures on the street.
Before long, many of their neighbors came and picked some
special things for themselves. Even Nasty Annie came.

Nasty Annie found a teacup which was even nicer than the one that had broken. Rebecca and Margaret looked on.

Finally, Rebecca could contain herself no longer. "You really are nasty, Annie!" she shouted.

"I'm not nasty!" Annie said. "You're the nasty ones. You don't care about me. You just care about your things. I'm going home."

After one last look, Margaret and Rebecca sadly started home. On their way up, they saw Nasty Annie sitting at her table, looking more miserable than ever.

"Poor Annie, alone with only a teacup," said Rebecca.
"And without even a saucer," said Margaret.

Margaret went back and found a saucer.

Rebecca and Margaret knocked at Annie's door. "We thought you might like this for your tea set," they said.

"You're not still angry?" Annie asked.

Rebecca and Margaret shook their heads.

"Well, I'm not, either," Annie whispered. "And, you know, I was thinking that vase would look stunning by our front door."

So, together, Rebecca, Margaret, and Nasty Annie carried the vase up the front steps and set it down.

Then they all went to Annie's and had a splendid tea.